Storybook Treasury for Girls

By Elizabeth Anders, Sonali Fry, Wendy Cheyette Lewison, Ann Morris, Emily Sollinger, and Debra Mostow Zakarin

Illustrated by Dawn Apperley, Judith Mitchell, Mary Morgan, Stacy Peterson, Nancy Sheehan, and Jerry Smath

GROSSET & DUNLAP

Table of Contents

I Wear My Tutu Everywhere!

By Wendy Cheyette Lewison
Illustrated by Mary Morgan

O nce there was a little girl named Tilly who loved to dance.

She danced while Mama was braiding her hair.
"Please hold still," said Mama.

She danced while she was brushing her teeth.

And she danced in her dreams.

So, when Tilly's birthday came around, Mama and Papa knew just what to give her for a present.

A tutu, a beautiful pink tutu to dance in—
just like a real ballerina!
It fit perfectly.

Tilly loved her new tutu. She loved it so much that she wore it wherever she went!

"*I love my tutu,*
I don't care,
I wear my tutu
everywhere!"

sang Tilly, as she danced down the aisles at the supermarket.
In the frozen-food section it was pretty chilly.
But Tilly didn't mind.

JUICE $1.00

ICE CREAM BARS $1.99

ICE CREAM $3.00

CHOCOLATE ICE CREAM $1.50

"I love my tutu,
I don't care,
I wear my tutu
everywhere!"

sang Tilly, as she bounced along on a hayride
with her family.

"You look silly, Tilly," said her brother, Billy.
But Tilly didn't mind.

"I love my tutu,
I don't care,
I wear my tutu
everywhere!"

sang Tilly at the zoo. Then she
relevé-ed for the elephants . . .

. . . jeté-ed for the giraffes . . .

. . . and plié-ed for the penguins.

She wore her tutu to school.

She wore her tutu at the pool.

She wore her tutu on the train.

She wore her tutu in the rain.

She even wore her tutu
at the playground.
"It's too frilly, Tilly," said
her best friend, Milly.
But Tilly didn't mind.
Until . . . RRR-R-I-P!
Uh-oh! Tilly DID mind that!

So Mama had to fix Tilly's tutu.
And while she fixed it, Tilly had to wear her shorts to Milly's house. Her shorts were not as fancy as her tutu. But it *was* easier to ride her trike.

She had to wear her party dress to Willy's
birthday party. Everybody told her how pretty
she looked.

And she had to wear her pajamas to bed. Her
pajamas were nice and soft to sleep in—not itchy
and scratchy like her tutu.

By morning, Mama had Tilly's tutu all fixed. It looked brand-new! But that wasn't the only surprise Mama had for Tilly.

"I know just the perfect place for you to wear your tutu," said Mama. "It isn't the supermarket. It isn't the zoo. It isn't the school and it isn't the pool."

It was dancing class!
And that's where Tilly went in her tutu every
week, so she could learn how to dance . . .

. . . just like a real ballerina.

Little Ballerinas

By Ann Morris
Photographs by Nancy Sheehan

Look what Emily can do! She learned it at ballet school. She is practicing in the kitchen to get ready for her class today. "I can dance, too!" says her little sister.

Rachel goes to the same ballet school. She is in Emily's class.
"Let's brush your hair into a ponytail," says Rachel's father.
"It will stay out of your way while you're dancing."

Julie can't wait to get to class. She even dances while she brushes her teeth.

Finally, off they all go to the studio. They carry their dance clothes and shoes in a special bag. They skip up the ramp. They skip through the door.

Inside they get into their leotards. Now they look like little ballerinas! First, they go to the *barre*, a long pole along the wall. At the *barre*, they do exercises to warm up and make their bodies strong.

The teacher helps them learn special dance steps and positions.

"Point your toe like this," she says. "Very good!"

"Now bend your knees. This is called a *plié*."

The teacher shows Marikka
how to turn her leg out.
"You did that so well," she says.
And she gives Marikka a big hug.

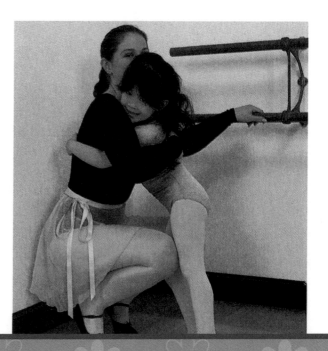

Good friends are made at ballet school.

They dance together . . .

and have fun together.

They help each other, too.
"Can you show me how to stretch?" asks Julie.
"Like this," says Emily.

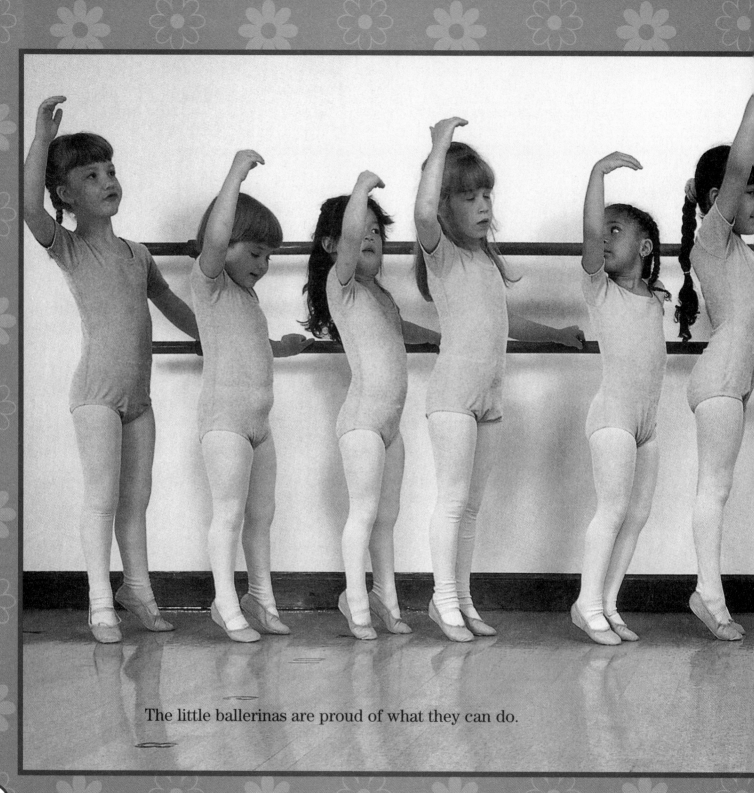

The little ballerinas are proud of what they can do.

They have worked very hard. Now they are ready
to put on a show.

On the day of the big performance, they get out their pretty pink tutus. . .

. . .and put them on.
"How do I look?" says Allison.

A little makeup will give their faces color under the bright stage lights. Some lipstick . . .

a touch of blush . . .

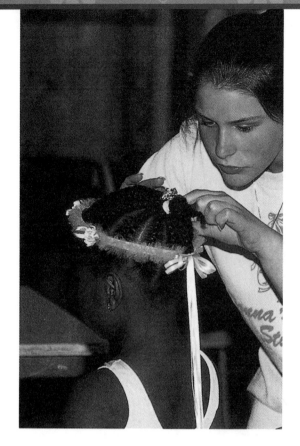

. . . and a beautiful crown with tiny pink flowers.

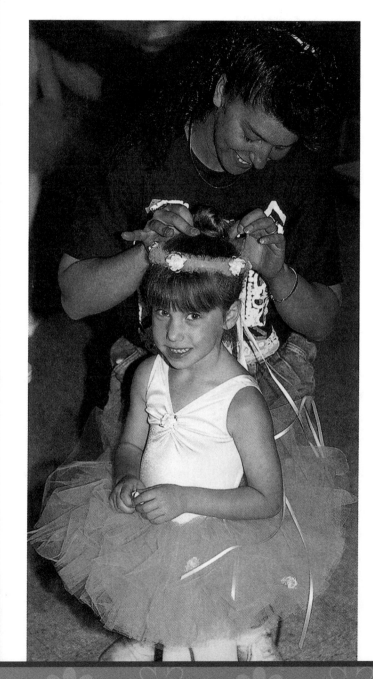

They feel very grown-up!

"Will I remember my steps?" thinks Nicole.

"Will they like my dance?" wonders Jessica.

The children are feeling happy and excited. Now they can show their parents and friends all the things they have learned!

The music begins. Each ballerina waits for her turn to go onstage.

They dance together.

They dance their very best.
They dance and dance!

When the show is over, they take a bow. Everyone claps.
"BRAVO!" they call out.
That means "Hooray! You were wonderful!"

The parents are proud of their little ballerinas. There are lots of pictures to be taken.

There are lots of hugs—
and lots of flowers, too!

Wouldn't you like
to be a ballerina?

Countdown to Grandma's House

By Debra Mostow Zakarin
Illustrated by Stacy Peterson

I'm going to Grandma's house. I really can't wait!
We will have a sleepover. Grandma and I will play all day long.
She always lets me stay up past my bedtime.

TO GRANDMA'S

I will count the days until I go to Grandma's house.
Why can't it be today?

Ten long days until I go to Grandma's house.
We will paint our fingernails. First we soak our
hands. Then Grandma will brush on the polish. I'll
choose ten different colors for each of my fingers.
"Cool," Grandma will say with a smile. Then I'll paint
my toes!

Nine days until I go to Grandma's house and to the park we'll go.

Along the way we'll jump like frogs, hop like bunnies, skip like best friends, and ride the Number 9 bus.

"Higher," I'll shout as Grandma pushes me on the swing. I wish it were today.

Eight more days until I go to Grandma's house. Then it will be dress-up time! I love all the clothes in Grandma's big closet. Grandma will look so silly with eight silk scarves all over her. We will have a pretend tea party!

Seven more days until I go to Grandma's house! We will plant some flowers in Grandma's garden. I'll press seven little seeds into the dirt. I'll water the plants and patiently wait for them to grow.

Six more days until I go to Grandma's house. We will cuddle together in her special chair. Grandma will read me my six favorite books. I like to rest my head on her shoulder and listen closely to the stories.

Five more days until I go to Grandma's house. Grandma and I will bake cookies. We will sift the flour. We will crack the eggs. Then we'll mix it up and put the cookie tray in the oven. Later, we'll take the steamy cookies out of the oven. Yummy.

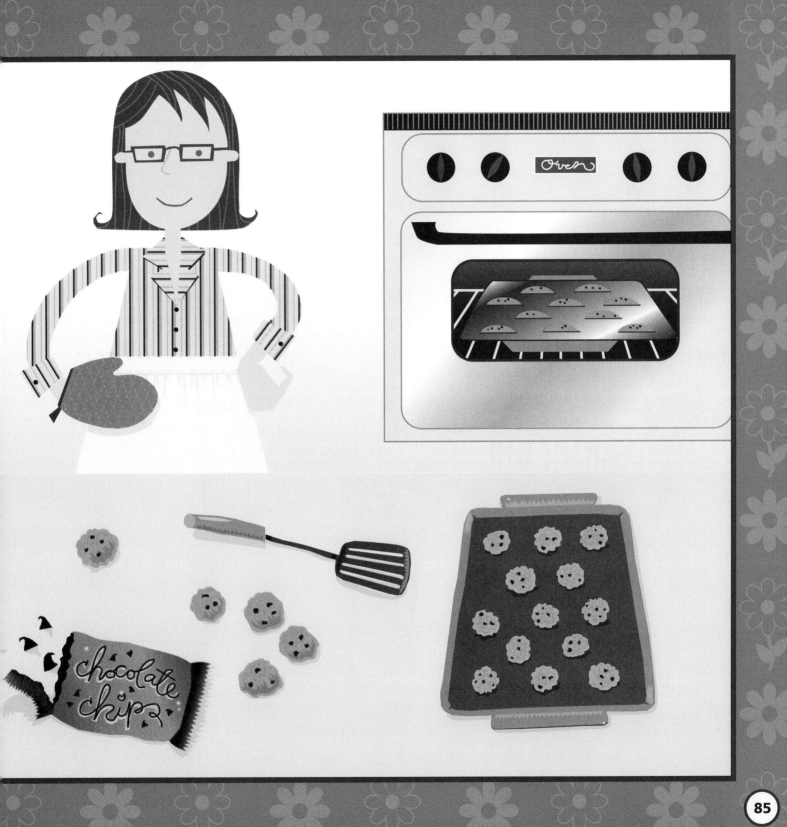

Four more days until I go to Grandma's house, and then I'll sing and dance. Grandma will play the piano and I will twirl around and around in my pink tutu. One step, two step, three step, and turn.

Three more days until I go to Grandma's house! After dinner we will walk to the ice-cream store. Three scoops for me, please. I will order a chocolate, bubble-gum, and mint-chip ice-cream cone. Grandma is an expert ice-cream eater. Her cone never drips like mine.

Two more days until I go to Grandma's house! We will play flashlight games under the covers. One flashlight for me and one flashlight for Grandma. We will click them on and off, on and off. Grandma and I won't be able to stop giggling.

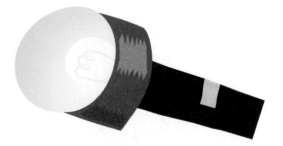

Only one more day till Grandma's house! I will run into her arms for a great big bear hug. "Grandma," I'll say. "Let's count all the fun things we will do together."

Oh, no! I really must pack.
One teddy bear. Two nightgowns.
Three pairs of shoes. Four long pants.

Five shirts.
Six bracelets.
Seven white undershirts.

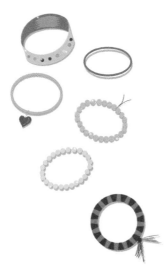

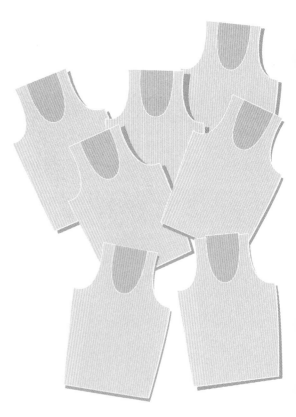

Eight belts.
Nine pairs of socks.
Ten hair ribbons.

I thought this day would never come!

The Best Tea Party Ever!

Written by Sonali Fry
Illustrated by Dawn Apperley

Sarina sat alone at the kitchen table. She was very unhappy.

"It wasn't supposed to rain today," she said to her mother. "I was going to play with my friends in the park. *Now* what am I going to do?"

Sarina's mother thought for a moment. "There are lots of things you can do," she said. "I know. Why don't you have a tea party?"

"A tea party?" asked Sarina.

"Sure," said her mother. "We can invite all your friends and make your favorite treats. It will be the best tea party ever!"

"That sounds like fun!" said Sarina.

So Sarina called her friends and invited them to the tea party. Then, she and her mom made a list of things they would need to buy from the grocery store.

At the grocery store, Sarina and her mom gathered all the items on their list. When they were done, the cart was full!

Back at home, they started to make the food for the tea party. Sarina and her mom put on aprons so their clothes wouldn't get dirty.

First, they made sandwiches. Sarina wanted peanut butter and jelly, because that was her favorite! Then it was time to make the desserts. They made all kinds of goodies— gingerbread cookies, star-shaped cookies, cupcakes, and more!

"Working together is so much fun!" said Sarina.

After the desserts were ready, they began to set the table.

"Oh, no!" said Sarina. "We forgot to buy paper cups and plates! And there's no time to go out and buy some!"

"Don't worry, Sarina," said her mother calmly. "I have a surprise for you. Let's go to the attic."

In the attic, Sarina's mom opened a large box. Inside were some objects wrapped in tissue paper. Sarina's mom took one out and unwrapped it. It was a beautiful teacup.

"This is the china that my mother gave me when I was your age," she said. "The entire set is here, and I've been saving it for you. If you're careful, you can use it today for your party."

"I promise I'll be careful," said Sarina. "Thanks, Mom!"

They carefully washed the china and placed it around the table with the food. Sarina's mom filled the teapot with fruit punch. But when the table was finally set, Sarina looked at it and frowned.

"I wish I had some flowers to put in the center," she said.

Sarina's mother had an idea. "There are plenty of pretty flowers in the garden. Why don't you go outside and pick some?"

"But it's raining," said Sarina.

"Come on, I'll help you," said her mother.

The garden was filled with beautiful flowers—roses, daisies, sunflowers, and more. Sarina picked the ones she liked and placed them in a basket. Her mother held an umbrella over them to keep the rain away.

After they picked the flowers, Sarina's mother looked at her watch.

"Oh, my!" she said. "It's time to get dressed. Your guests will be here any minute!"

Sarina ran to her room and tried to choose some clothes and jewelry. She was so excited, she couldn't decide what to wear!

Suddenly, the doorbell rang. Her guests had arrived!

Sarina greeted her friends and took them to the table. But just as they were about to sit down, she noticed that it wasn't raining anymore.

"Look! The sun is coming out!" she said happily.

Her mother looked out the window. "Now we can have the party outside," she said.

The party was moved to the garden, and it was now a beautiful, sunny day. Sarina took the china teapot and filled everyone's cup. The girls ate tasty sandwiches, yummy cookies, and delicious cupcakes. Everyone had a wonderful time.

Sarina gave her mom a big hug. "Thanks for everything, Mom."
"Are you having a good time?" she asked.
"Of course I am. This is the best tea party ever!" said Sarina.

Jewel Fairies

by Emily Sollinger
Illustrated by Judith Mitchell

Meet the Jewel Fairies! They live in Fairyland. Each fairy wears a special, beautiful jewel.

Every fairy has glittery wings on her back
that open up wide when she flies through
the air to visit her other Jewel Fairy friends.

Ruby Fairy lives high up in the mountains where the leaves on the trees are orange and red. Her bright, square-shaped ruby earrings shine in the sun. She wears a red dress that shimmers when she moves.

Emerald Fairy lives in the deep, green forest, where there are magic frogs and plants that can talk. Her sparkling green emerald ring glistens each time she waves her arm to cast a magic fairy spell.

Diamond Fairy lives where icicles grow on trees and sparkly snowflakes fall all year round. When she wears her diamond tiara and sings her own secret song, she can turn any ordinary rock into a sparkling diamond!

Sapphire Fairy lives on a sailboat that floats along the blue ocean waves. Her wand is covered with magic blue sapphires that guide her boat.

Though they live in different places, the fairies are all very good friends. When they visit each other, they love to dance and sing fairy songs. When the Jewel Fairies get together, there is always magic in the air! They can't wait to see each other again.

One morning, the Jewel Fairy Queen sends out a very important note to each fairy. It says that there is a special surprise! A new Jewel Fairy is coming. Who could she be?

Later that day, each fairy finds the note in her magic mailbox. The fairies are excited! They can't wait to meet her, and give her a very special welcome at the party the Queen is planning.

The next day is the day of the party. The Jewel Fairies can hardly wait! Each fairy spends the morning getting dressed and ready.

Diamond Fairy is putting satin bows in her hair. She wants to look her sparkliest for the party!

Sapphire Fairy is almost ready to go! All she needs to do now is lace up her shiny blue shoes.

At the palace, the fairies are greeted by
The Queen and the new fairy, Pearl.
Her pearl necklace is pink and shiny.

Each fairy gives Pearl her own special jewel to wear for the day. They hold hands and dance around her. They sing the fairy welcome song.

At the end of the day, Pearl Fairy gives each sparkling
jewel back to its owner.
"Thank you for making me feel so welcome!"
"That's what being a fairy is all about!" they reply.

The
Flower Princesses

By Elizabeth Anders
Illustrated by Jerry Smath

ome stand on tiptoe and peek into this magic garden.
Maybe you will see the Flower Princesses!

There they are—Princess Buttercup, Princess Hyacinth, Princess Iris, Princess Lily, Princess Tulip, and Princess Rose. Can you see them playing in the grass? They are as tiny as fairies!

The Flower Princesses love to laugh
and sing and play games together.

But each princess has something special she likes to do, all by herself.

Princess Buttercup, in her bright yellow dress, likes to skip to the meadow. There, she runs and plays with the butterflies, gathering buttercups until her basket is full.

Princess Hyacinth sits in a berry bush, drinking from dewdrops and listening to the bluebirds sing.

Princess Iris has a peapod canoe. She paddles around the fountain all day long, splashing as she goes.

Princess Lily likes to spend her days at the pond. Watch her leap across the lily pads, playing tag with the frogs!

Princess Tulip is a dancer. She whirls and twirls on her tiny feet, moving to the music of the wind.

Last is Princess Rose, riding a dragonfly through the air. She swoops and glides over the garden, waving to her sisters.

When the day is almost over, and the sun is starting to set, it is time for the Flower Princesses to have a tea party.

As the moon and stars come out, the Flower
Princesses go to sleep in their little flower beds.

Now, what do you think Flower Princesses dream about?